ONLY ONE NEIGHBORHOOD

BY *Marc Harshman* & *Barbara Garrison*

ILLUSTRATED BY BARBARA GARRISON

DUTTON CHILDREN'S BOOKS

For all my neighbors, past and present—peace. ⬟ **M.H.**   For Dylan and Daniel ⬟ **B.G.**

DUTTON CHILDREN'S BOOKS
A DIVISION OF PENGUIN YOUNG READERS GROUP

Published by the Penguin Group

Penguin Group (USA) Inc., 375 Hudson Street, New York, New York 10014, U.S.A.

Penguin Group (Canada), 90 Eglinton Avenue East, Suite 700, Toronto, Ontario, Canada M4P 2Y3 (a division of Pearson Penguin Canada Inc.)

Penguin Books Ltd, 80 Strand, London WC2R 0RL, England

Penguin Ireland, 25 St Stephen's Green, Dublin 2, Ireland (a division of Penguin Books Ltd)

Penguin Group (Australia), 250 Camberwell Road, Camberwell, Victoria 3124, Australia (a division of Pearson Australia Group Pty Ltd)

Penguin Books India Pvt Ltd, 11 Community Centre, Panchsheel Park, New Delhi - 110 017, India

Penguin Group (NZ), 67 Apollo Drive, Rosedale, North Shore 0745, Auckland, New Zealand (a division of Pearson New Zealand Ltd)

Penguin Books (South Africa) (Pty) Ltd, 24 Sturdee Avenue, Rosebank, Johannesburg 2196, South Africa

Penguin Books Ltd, Registered Offices: 80 Strand, London WC2R 0RL, England

LIBRARY OF CONGRESS CATALOGING-IN-PUBLICATION DATA

Harshman, Marc.

Only one neighborhood / Marc Harshman ; Barbara Garrison. — 1st ed.

p. cm.

Summary: Explores a neighborhood that has only one of several kinds of buildings, but within each there are many things, such as different kinds of breads in the bakery, then shows that the neighborhood itself is just one of many in a world united by a single wish.

ISBN 978-0-525-47468-5 (hardcover)

[1. Neighborhood—Fiction. 2. City and town life—Fiction.] I. Garrison, Barbara, ill. II. Title.

PZ7.H256247Onl 2007   [E]—dc22   2006035908

Published in the United States by Dutton Children's Books,

a division of Penguin Young Readers Group, 345 Hudson Street, New York, New York 10014 www.penguin.com/youngreaders

Designed by Heather Wood ‡ Manufactured in China ‡ First Edition

1 3 5 7 9 10 8 6 4 2

⬟ **ART NOTE** ⬟

The art for this book is a series of collagraphs, a word that comes from "collage" and "graphic." The artist begins with a heavy piece of smooth cardboard. Pieces of paper of different textures, fabric, string, and even feathers are glued in layers on the cardboard "plate" to form the image. Some smooth areas of the cardboard may be cut and peeled away. Gesso is painted over the entire plate, adding additional texture and definition. Several coats of acrylic medium are then applied and allowed to dry thoroughly.

Next, the artist prints her collagraphs "intaglio." Ink is spread over the entire plate. The surface ink is wiped off. The plate is placed face up on an etching press and covered with a damp 100% rag paper. Felt blankets are placed on top and the plate is passed through the press.

Finally, watercolor washes are added to each individual print.

There may be only one neighborhood,
but there is so much in it.

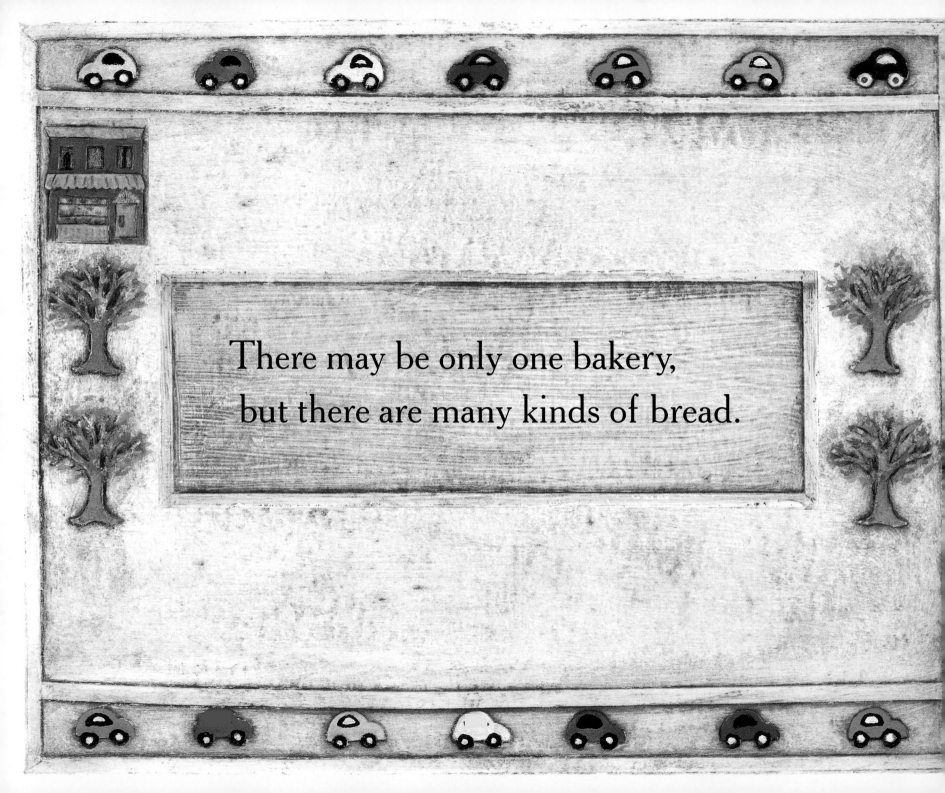

There may be only one bakery,
but there are many kinds of bread.

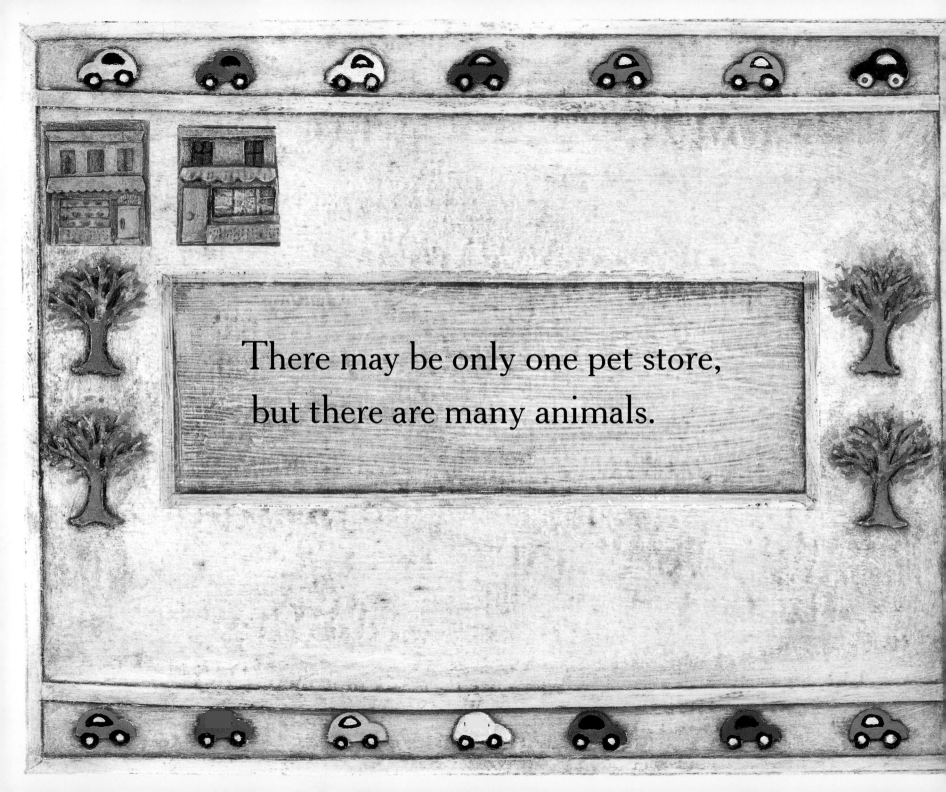

There may be only one pet store,
but there are many animals.

There may be only one toy store,
but there are many toys.

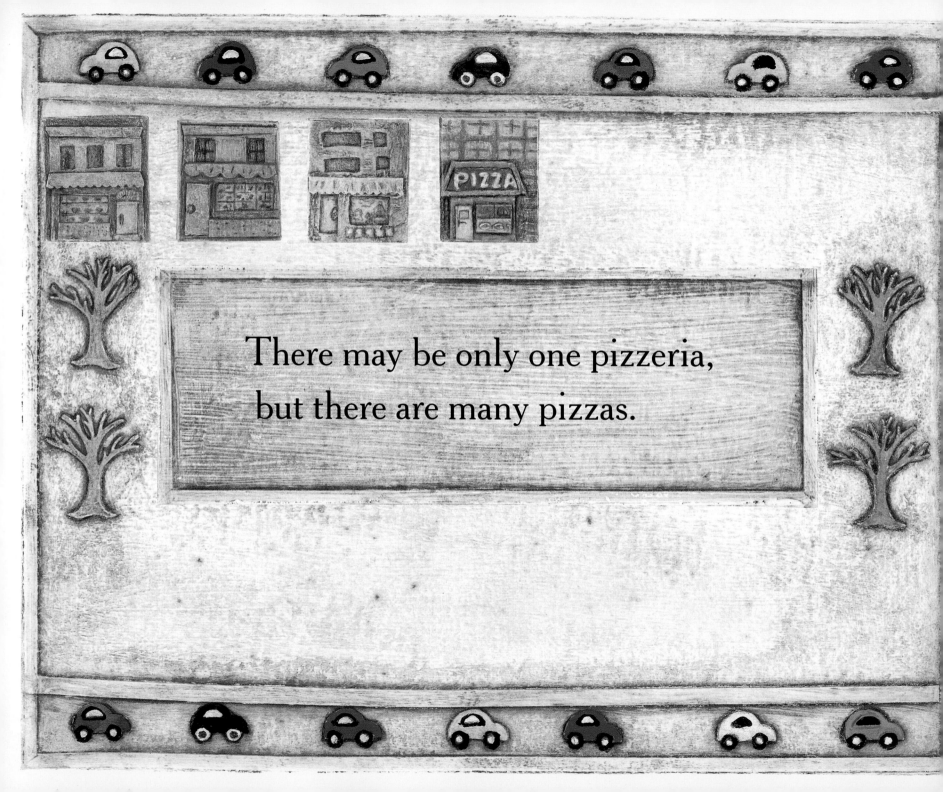

There may be only one pizzeria,
but there are many pizzas.

There may be only one market,
but there are many vegetables.

There may be only one shoe store,
but there are many shoes.

There may be only one hardware store,
but there are many tools.

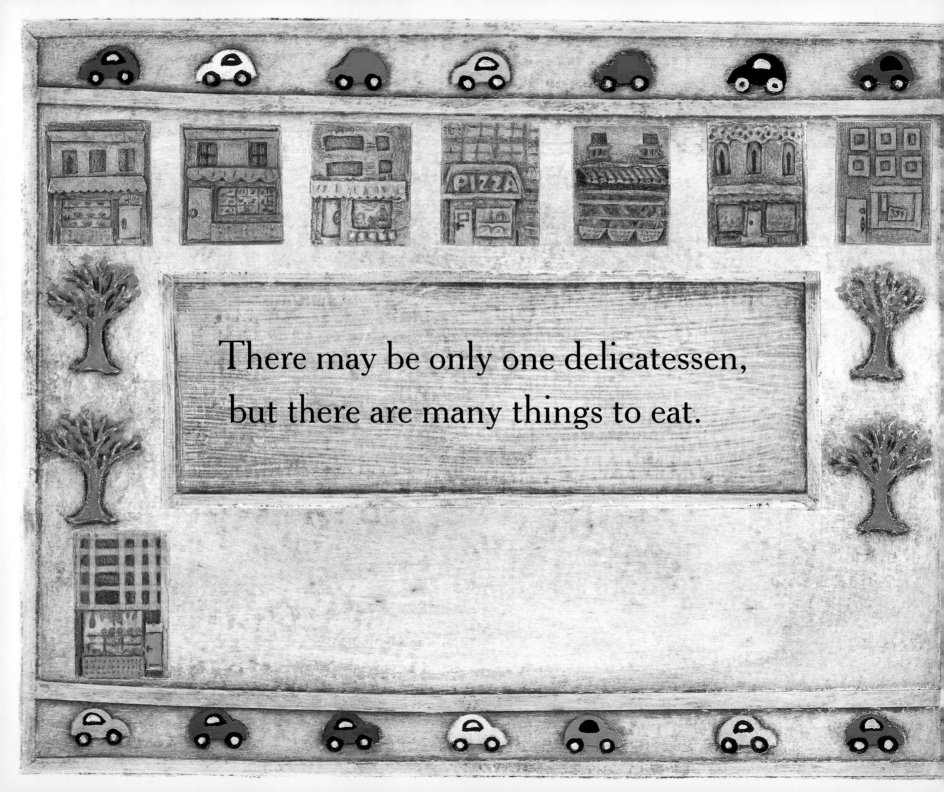

There may be only one delicatessen,
but there are many things to eat.

There may be only one music store,
but there are many instruments.

There may be only one flower shop,
but there are many flowers.

There may be only one firehouse,
but there are many boots, hats, and coats.

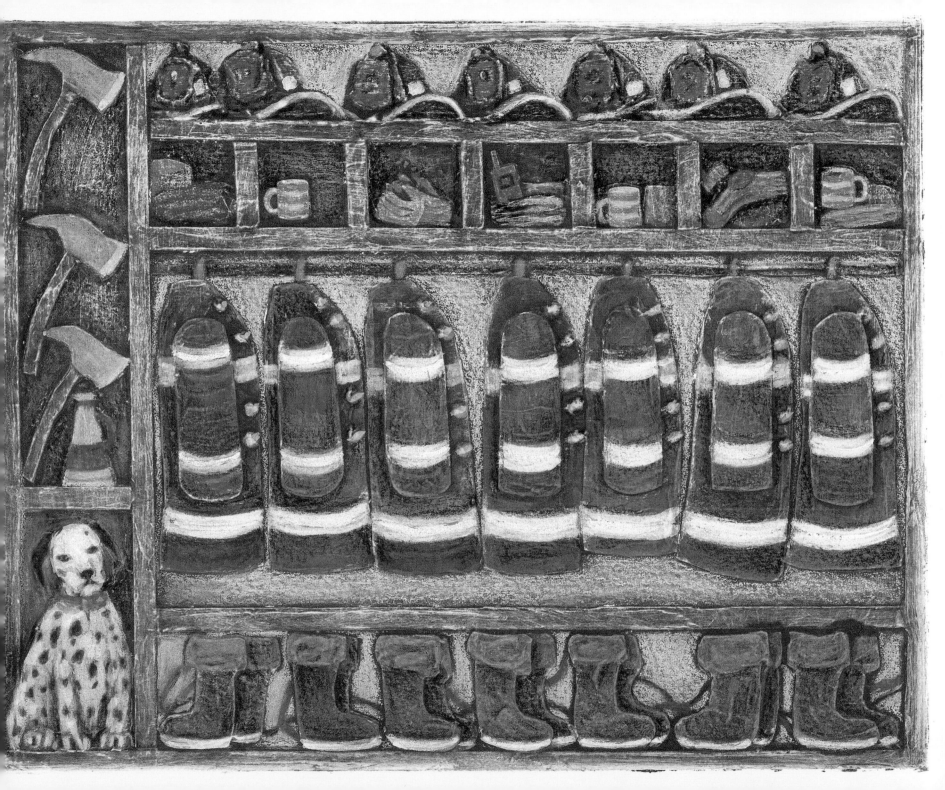

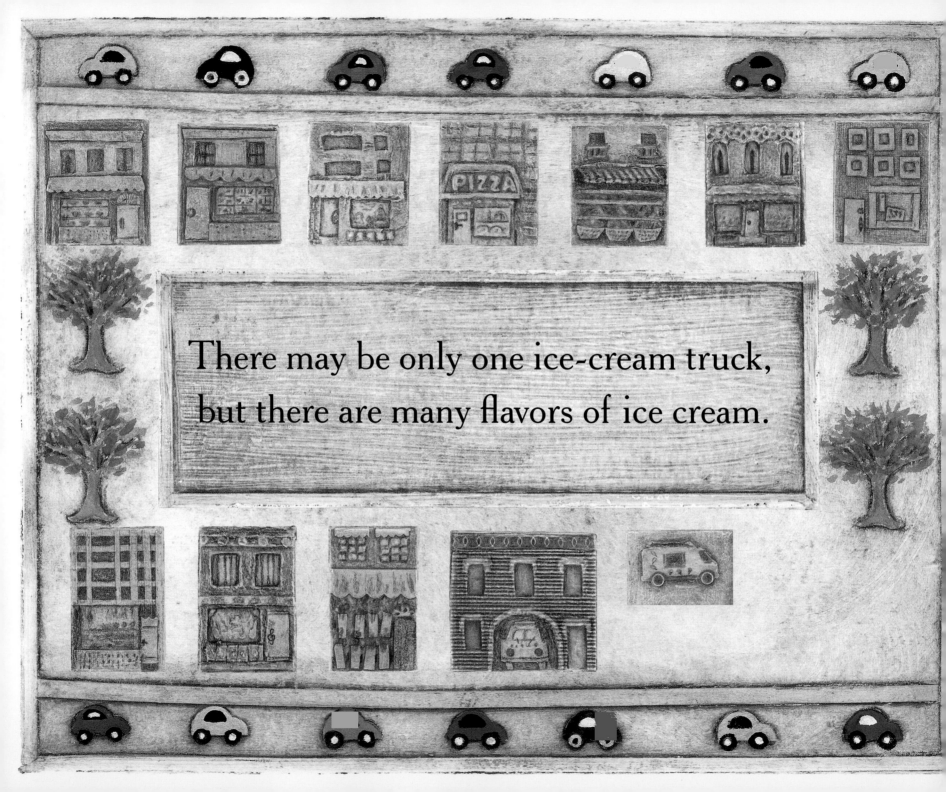

There may be only one ice-cream truck, but there are many flavors of ice cream.

There may be only one school,
but there are many children.

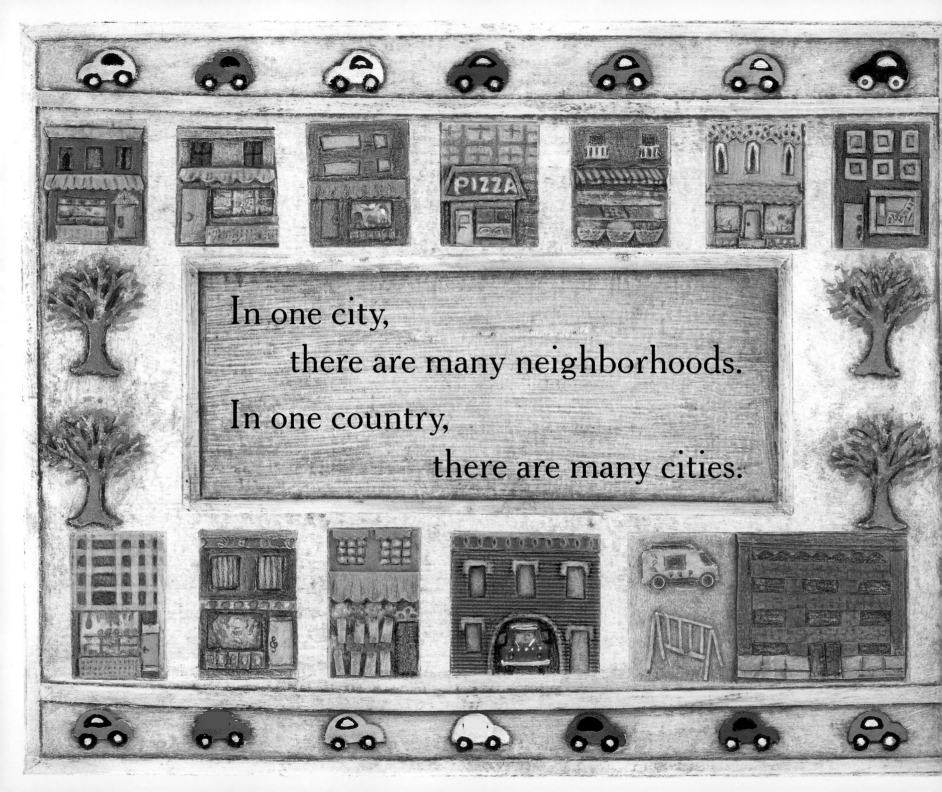

In one city,
     there are many neighborhoods.
In one country,
          there are many cities.

In one world, there are many countries.
But there is only one wish: P E A C E.